Here We Go Round the Mulberry Bush

the Mulberry Bush

As told and illustrated by Iza Trapani

Charle

Published by Charlesbridge
85 Main Street
Watertown, MA 02472
(617) 926-0329
www.charlesbridge.com

Library of Congress Cataloging-in-Publication Data
Trapani, Iza.
Here we go 'round the mulberry bush / written and illustrated by Iza Trapani.
p. cm.
Summary: An expansion of the traditional song which features a battle
between a gardener and some "pesky critters" in search of a snack.
ISBN-13: 978-1-57091-663-2; ISBN-10: 1-57091-663-2 (reinforced for library use)
ISBN-13: 978-1-57091-699-1; ISBN-10: 1-57091-699-3 (softcover)
1. Children's songs, English—United States—Texts. [1. Gardening—Songs and music.
2. Pests—Songs and music. 3. Songs.] I. Title.
PZ8.3.T686Her   2006
782.42164'0268—dc22
[E]   2005019617

Printed in Singapore
(hc) 10 9 8 7 6 5 4 3 2 1
(sc) 10 9 8 7 6 5 4 3 2 1

Illustrations done in watercolor on Arches 300-pound coldpress watercolor paper
Display type and text type set in Whimsy and Horley
Color separated by Chroma Graphics, Singapore
Printed and bound by Imago
Production supervision by Brian G. Walker
Designed by Diane M. Earley

For Ava Grace, who is everyone's sunshine!
With love, Iza

Here we go 'round the mulberry bush,
The mulberry bush, the mulberry bush.
Here we go 'round the mulberry bush,
So early in the morning.

Out of my garden—keep away!
Leave right now without delay.
Pests are not invited to stay,
So listen to my warning.

Oh, how I love to dig and hoe,
Scatter my seeds row by row,
Water them well and watch them grow
In spring when sunshine's glowing.

Oh, how we love to pull up roots,
Nibble on fresh and tender shoots,
Fill up on plump and juicy fruits,
In spring when plants are growing.

Didn't I say, "Do not return!"?
Those pesky critters have no concern.
I'll put up a fence and then they'll learn
I really mean good-bye.

In through the holes we slink inside.
Under the peas and lettuce we hide.
We're very teeny and can't be spied
While snacking on the sly.

Netting will surely do the trick.
I'll lay it on so nice and thick.
Stop those little skulkers quick
And make them go away.

Under the fence we tunnel through.
Broccoli! Beans! A dream come true!
Oh, how we love to chomp and chew
And gobble here all day.

I'll dig a trench that goes around,
Then add some fencing underground.
Send those gluttons homeward bound.
There's no way they'll get under.

Out in the field we leap and hop,
Up to the fence and over the top.
What a delicious bumper crop
To raid and loot and plunder!

This is my last and final try.
I'll build a fence that's really high.
Keep all those crooks from dropping by
And teach them to stay clear.

Open the gate, and we're in luck.
Corn on the cob, ready to pluck.
Oh, how we love to pick and shuck
All night when no one's here.

Here we go 'round the mulberry bush,
The mulberry bush, the mulberry bush.
Here we go 'round the mulberry bush.
'Round and 'round each year!

Here We Go 'Round the Mulberry Bush

Here we go 'round the mul-ber-ry bush, the mul-ber-ry bush, the mul-ber-ry bush.

Here we go 'round the mul-ber-ry bush, so ear-ly in ___ the morn - ing.

Out of my garden—keep away!
Leave right now without delay.
Pests are not invited to stay,
So listen to my warning.

Oh, how I love to dig and hoe,
Scatter my seeds row by row,
Water them well and watch them grow
In spring when sunshine's glowing.

Oh, how we love to pull up roots,
Nibble on fresh and tender shoots,
Fill up on plump and juicy fruits,
In spring when plants are growing.

Didn't I say, "Do not return!"?
Those pesky critters have no concern.
I'll put up a fence and then they'll learn
I really mean good-bye.

In through the holes we slink inside.
Under the peas and lettuce we hide.
We're very teeny and can't be spied
While snacking on the sly.

Netting will surely do the trick.
I'll lay it on so nice and thick.
Stop those little skulkers quick
And make them go away.

Under the fence we tunnel through.
Broccoli! Beans! A dream come true!
Oh, how we love to chomp and chew
And gobble here all day.

I'll dig a trench that goes around,
Then add some fencing underground.
Send those gluttons homeward bound.
There's no way they'll get under.

Out in the field we leap and hop,
Up to the fence and over the top.
What a delicious bumper crop
To raid and loot and plunder!

This is my last and final try.
I'll build a fence that's really high.
Keep all those crooks from dropping by
And teach them to stay clear.

Open the gate, and we're in luck.
Corn on the cob, ready to pluck.
Oh, how we love to pick and shuck
All night when no one's here.

Here we go 'round the mulberry bush,
The mulberry bush, the mulberry bush.
Here we go 'round the mulberry bush.
'Round and 'round each year!